The **Big** I

Written by Fiona Tomlinson
Illustrated by Omar Aranda

Collins

Ben picks a nut.

Fin picks a big nut.

Ben raps the nut.

Fin raps the big nut.

Ben taps the nut.

Fin taps the big nut.

Ben kicks the nut.

Fin kicks the big nut.

The big nut hits Hen.

Hen huffs, puffs and tuts.

Hen picks up the nut.

Hen pecks at the nut.

/f/

14

ff

15

After reading

Letters and Sounds: Phase 2

Word count: 56

Focus phonemes: /g/ /k/ /e/ /u/ /r/ /h/ /b/ /f/, ff, ck

Common exception words: the, and

Curriculum links: Understanding the World

Early learning goals: Reading: use phonic knowledge to decode regular words and read them aloud accurately; demonstrate understanding when talking with others about what they have read

Developing fluency

- Encourage your child to sound talk and then blend the words, e.g. /n/ /u/ /t/. It may help to point to each sound as your child reads.
- Then ask your child to reread the sentence to support fluency and understanding.
- You could reread the whole book to your child to model fluency and rhythm in the story.

Phonic practice

- Ask your child to sound talk and blend each of the following words: k/i/ck, p/i/ck, h/u/ff, p/u/ff
- Ask them to point to the words that have a ck in them. (*picks*, *kicks*, *pecks*)
- Look at the "I spy sounds" pages (14–15). Discuss the picture with your child. Can they find items/ examples of words containing /f/ or ff? (e.g. *fish, fin, puff, huff, four, fly, fur, frizzy fur, cliff*)

Extending vocabulary

- The words **huff**, **puff** and **tut** are sounds we make to complain or show disapproval. What other words describe how someone sounds when they complain? (e.g. *grumble, groan, moan, grunt, growl, gasp, sigh, whine, whimper*)
- Ask your child to have a go at making the following noises: **huff**, **puff**, **grunt**, **sigh**, **tut**, **whine**, **whimper**, **moan**, **squeak** and **squeal**. You could model the noises too.